W9-BRI-611

To Maeve Benigna Grogan
—J.G.

Welcome, Daisy Mae!
—R.C.

Trick or Treat, Marley!
Copyright © 2011 by John Grogan
All rights reserved. Manufactured in China.
No part of this book may be used or reproduced in any manner whatsoever without written
permission except in the case of brief quotations embodied in critical articles and reviews. For
information address HarperCollins Children's Books, a division of HarperCollins Publishers,
10 East 53rd Street, New York, NY 10022.
www.harpercollinschildrens.com

Library of Congress Cataloging-in-Publication Data
Grogan, John, date.
    Trick or treat, Marley! / John Grogan ; illustrated by Richard Cowdrey. — 1st ed.
        p.   cm. — (Marley)
    Summary: Marley the high-spirited puppy tries to help his family with a Halloween party.
    ISBN 978-0-06-185755-3 (trade bdg,)
    [1. Dogs—Fiction. 2. Halloween—Fiction. 3. Animals—Infancy—Fiction.] I. Cowdrey,
Richard, ill. II. Title.
PZ7.G892564Tri 2011   2010017841
[E]—dc22   CIP
                                                            AC

Typography by Jeanne L. Hogle
11 12 13 14 15 SCP 10 9 8 7 6 5 4 3 2 1
❖
First Edition

By the #1 *New York Times* Bestselling Author

John Grogan

Trick or Treat, Marley!

illustrated by Richard Cowdrey

HARPER

An Imprint of HarperCollinsPublishers

Oh, I can't wait! I can't wait!" Cassie bubbled as she raced through the house, clutching her costume.

"Me no wait, too!" Baby Louie agreed. "Me Stupeman!"

Today was October 31, and they knew what that meant: Halloween! And this Halloween would be extra special because Mommy and Daddy and Cassie and Baby Louie were throwing a fun and spooky party with all their friends.

"Can we get in our costumes now?" Cassie asked. "Please, please, please?"

"Heavens no!" Mommy said with a laugh. "The party doesn't start for four more hours. First we have to get everything ready."

"Me help!" Baby Louie squealed.

"Woof! Woof!" said their big yellow puppy, Marley.

"Look!" Cassie said, pointing.
"Marley wants to help, too."

"First up, let's carve the pumpkin," Mommy said. She carried in the big orange gourd that Daddy had grown in the garden. With a crayon, Cassie drew a scary face. Then Mommy carefully cut the top off. "Okay, kids, dig in!" she said, and Cassie and Baby Louie reached inside the pumpkin and began scooping out its seeds and gooey guts.

"Ooh, squishy!"
Cassie squealed.

"Yuck-yuck!"
Baby Louie yelled.

Marley wanted to feel the goo, too. He kept trying to stick his head in the hole, but he couldn't quite fit.

"Waddy, go way!" Baby Louie said.

But Marley would not give up. He stuck his snout in the hole and pushed and pushed until— *pop!*—in went his head. *Whoa! Dark in here!*

Now Marley had a new problem. His head was stuck.

As much as he pried and pulled and rocked and rolled, he could not yank it free. So Marley did what Marley did best: He took off running.

"Marley! Come back with that pumpkin!"
Mommy scolded.

But Marley charged ahead blindly, not stopping until he ran straight into the wall. *Thunk!* The pumpkin split wide open. Out came Marley's head, covered in orange slime. He wiggled with joy as if to say, *Now, THAT was fun!*

"Good thing Daddy grew more than one pumpkin," Mommy said with a sigh.

The kids blew up balloons. Marley jumped and snapped at every one. *Pop! Pop!* they went.

Cassie and Baby Louie hung streamers. Marley turned them into confetti.

They draped the stairs
in creepy spiderwebs.
Marley swept them up
with his tail.

They pinned a scary skeleton to the
wall. Marley ran off with its leg bone.
"Bah boo boo, Waddy!" Baby Louie
scolded.

"That's it!" Mommy said. "You're in the doghouse, Buster." And she led him away.

"Decorating sure goes fast without Marley here to help," Cassie said.

BOO!

Finally, Mommy and the children had the house all ready for the party. Cassie and Baby Louie put on their costumes and waited for the doorbell to ring. Soon their friends began to arrive. There was a bumblebee, a ghost, a pirate, a football player, a scarecrow, and a princess. There was even a space alien. "Happy Halloween!" everyone shouted.

"Let the fun begin!" Cassie announced.

"Woof! Woof!" said Marley, as if to say, *I'm back just in time.*

Daddy looked sternly at the bouncing dog. "Marley, I'm giving you a second chance, but I expect you to be on your best behavior."

The kids bobbed for apples.
Marley bobbed, too.

The kids played Pin the Tail on the Donkey. Until, that is, you-know-who thought it would be much more fun to play Steal the Tail from the Donkey.

The kids didn't take pony rides, but they did the next best thing.

When they had a big popcorn fight, Marley volunteered for cleanup duty.

"Okay, kids," Mommy called out. "It's time for the treasure hunt. See how many pieces of candy you can find hidden

The children searched under the couches and above the shelf. They looked beneath pillows and behind chairs.

They found exactly ZERO! A certain someone with a super-sniffer nose had gotten there before them.

What Marley didn't know was sometimes you can get too much of a good thing.

"Waddy have tummy ache!" Baby Louie said.

A minute later, the children started to scream.
They shrieked at the top of their lungs. A spooky white ghost filled
the window and was banging against the glass. The ghost shook and
bounced and quivered. It let loose a spine-shivering moan.

"It's trying to get in!" one boy yelled.

"Run for your lives!" a girl screamed.

"What on earth?" Daddy said.

Then he spotted a clue. This ghost had a tail!

And so went the night. Everyone had fun, but no one had more
fun than Marley. And then it was time to go door-to-door through
the neighborhood, trick-or-treating. All the children lined up
behind Mommy and Daddy with their flashlights.

"Sorry, Marley, you have to stay home," Mommy said.
"Man the fort!" Daddy added.
And for once, Marley didn't mind being left behind.
He knew he had the most important job of all.

"Trick or treat,
Marley!"